www.ingramcontent.com/pod-product-compliance
Lightning Source LLC
Chambersburg PA
CBHW040847010826
48978CB00012BB/933

PROJECT
100

PROJECT 100 READS FROM RIGHT TO LEFT, STARTING IN THE UPPER RIGHT CORNER. JAPANESE IS READ FROM RIGHT TO LEFT, MEANING THAT ACTION SOUND EFFECTS AND WORD BALLOON ORDER ARE COMPLETELY REVERSED FROM ENGLISH ORDER.

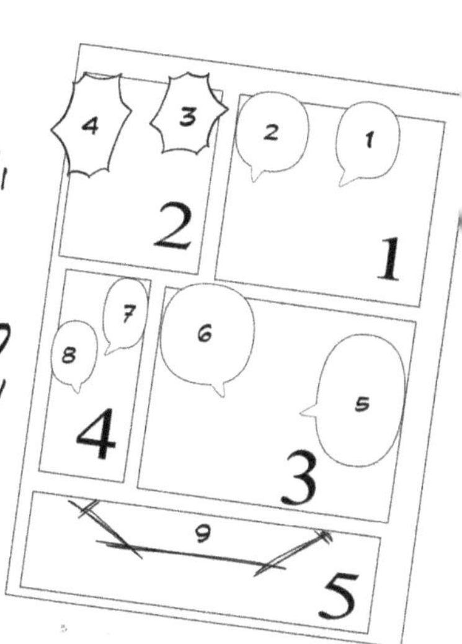

YEAH, MY NAME IS
NICHOLI BREITLING
THIS IS APOLLO
AND THIS IS ATLAS
TO BE CONTINUED...

HEY THERE!

Oakwood Elementary
LET'S GO! LET'S GO!
MMM

OH HI! DROPPING THEM OFF FOR THEIR FIRST DAY?

CAN I GET YOUR FIRST AND LAST NAME AS WELL THEIRS?
OH I BET IT IS!
CHECK IN TIME
Child's Guardian Name:

YEAH! IT'S QUITE A BIG DAY FOR THEM!

VROOM

AYE! Y'ALL BETTER SIT BACK DOWN

OHHH THE CLOUDS LOOK SO COOL!
WAIT I WANNA SEE TOO!

ALMOST THERE GUYS

EGHHH NOOOO~
I AM!

YOU'LL BE OKAY~. I KNOW YOU WILL

ALRIGHT LET'S GET A MOVING!

WE ALL GOOD TO GO?
YEAHHH!

ALRIGHT GO AND MUCH UP SOME FOOD.

AND CLOSE YOU'RE MOUTH WHEN YOU CHEW!

*GOBBLE *GOBBLE
HEY SLOW DOWN BUD

YOU GUY'S EXCITED FOR SCHOOL?

HAHA THATS RIGHT

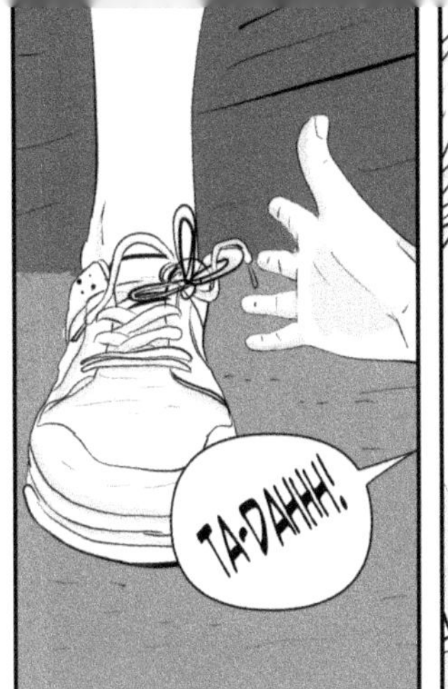

TA-DAHHH!

EH-...

IT'S OKA
I ALREADY TIED THEM!

THAT'S NOT QUITE RIGHT BUDDY
WHATTT! BUT I WATCHED YOU DO IT THE OTHER DAY!

HAHAH

JUST KEEP PRACTICING AND YOU'LL GET IT
HAHA YEAH BUT YOU GOTTA USE THE BUNNY EARS TECHNIQUE REMEMBER? IT'S THE EASIEST

NU-UH
I BET I CAN FINISH BEFORE YOU
*BRUSH *BRUSH

YEAH! GIMME A SEC!
DAD, CAN YOU COME TIE MY SHOES!?

ERGHH

WAIT LEMME DO IT! I LEARNED HOW TO DO TIE SHOES LIKE A PRO!
EHHH...

ERRR
ALSO CHANGE INTO YOUR SCHOOL CLOTHES!
WELL YOU'RE GONNA HAVE TO SO HURRY UP IMA COOK UP SOME FOOD
I DON'T WANNA GOOO
I'M NOT!
C'MON DON'T BE A BABY!
YESSSS PANCAKES!

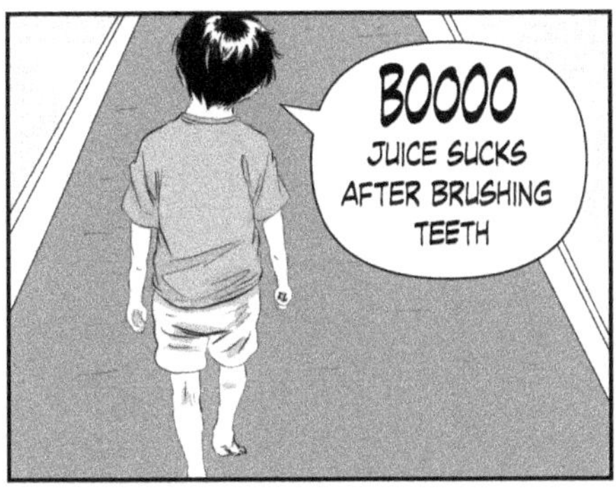

BOOOO
JUICE SUCKS AFTER BRUSHING TEETH

NO WAY YOU BRUSHED THOSE TEETH YET

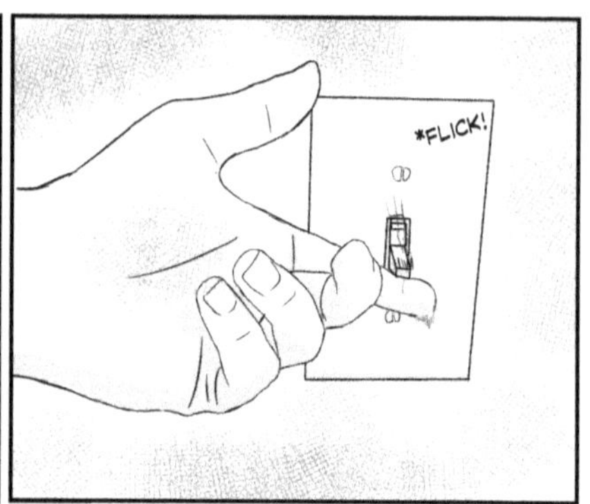
*FLICK!

OWWWW!
AHHGRGHH!

TIME TO WAKE UP GUYS!

IT'S FINALLY THE DAY!

WAIT

*BRUSH
BRUSH*

*CLICK

PROJECT 100
BY ERIK SUASTE

chapter 9:
our first day

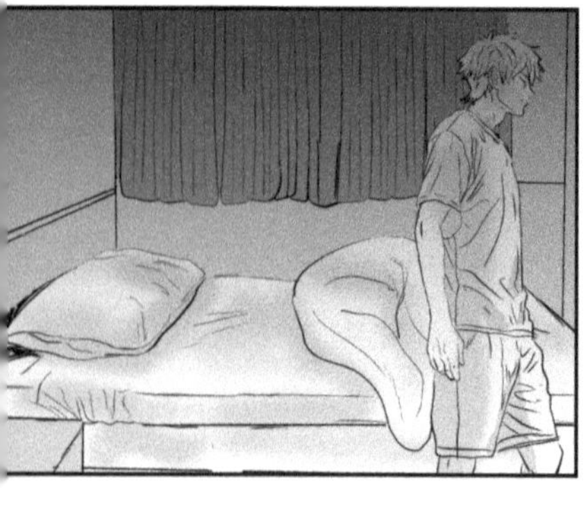

6

years later

Prologue
Fin

I WON'T FORGET YOU
I PROMISE

I WON'T FORGET YOU

HMMPH-

I WON'T FORGET YOU

WAHH!-
...
MMGHMM

WAHHH

WHERE ARE YA?
WAHHH

I'LL BE RIGHT BACK

IM HERE

WAHHH..

WAHHH!
I GOTCHA

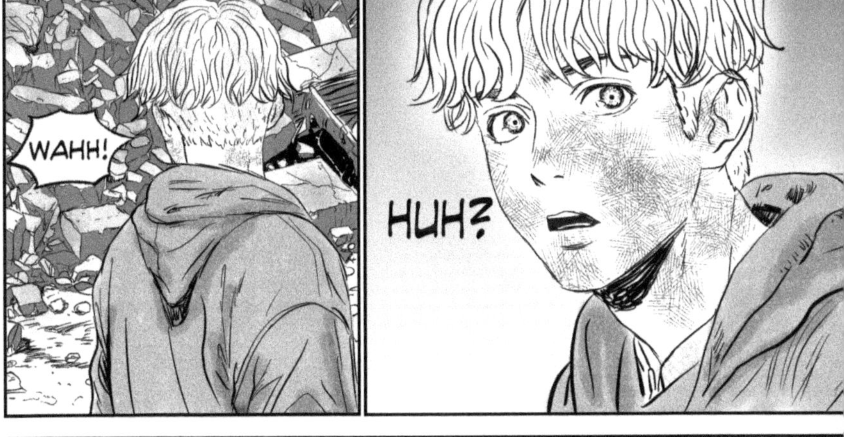

WAHH!
HUH?

ANOTHER ONE!?

WAHHH!

WAH
H!

...

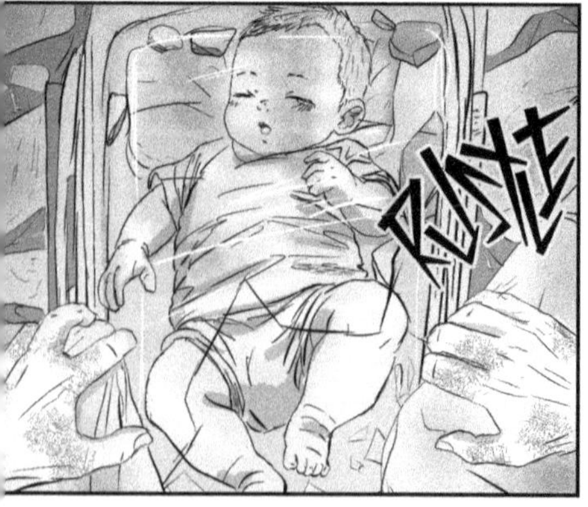

RUSTLE

THERE!

...
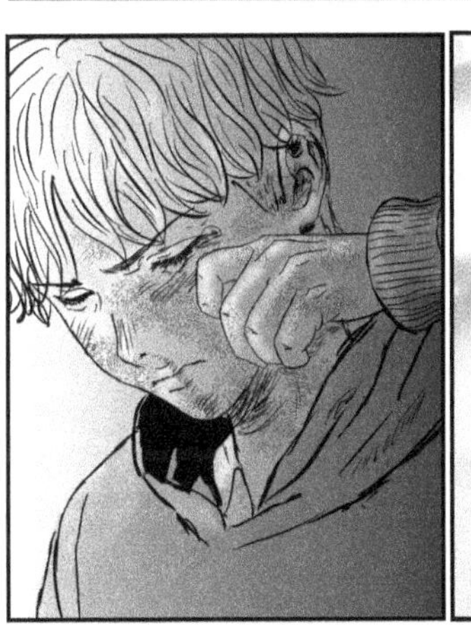

WAHHH!

...I WISH
HEHH... HGHH...
I COULD STAY WITH YOU

IT WON'T BE LONG BEFORE MORE OF PHOENIX COMES

I CANT JUST LEAVE YOU HERE

AND... I'VE LOST TOO MUCH BLOOD ALREADY...

..PLEASE MAKE SURE THEY'RE SAFE... THEY DIDN'T DESERVE ANY OF THIS...

... I NEED YOU TO DO ONE LAST THING FOR ME NICHOLI...

...PLEASE
WE HAVE
TO GET
YOU OUT
OF HERE
FIRST

MARI

YOU HAVE
TO HELP
THAT CRY

NICHOLI...
YOU HAVE
TO MAKE
SURE THEY
CAN SEE
TOMORROW
TOO

FWOOSH
FWOOSH

WAHHH

COO~
COO~

NICHOLI... THERES STILL A BABY ALIVE

DID YOU HEAR THAT?

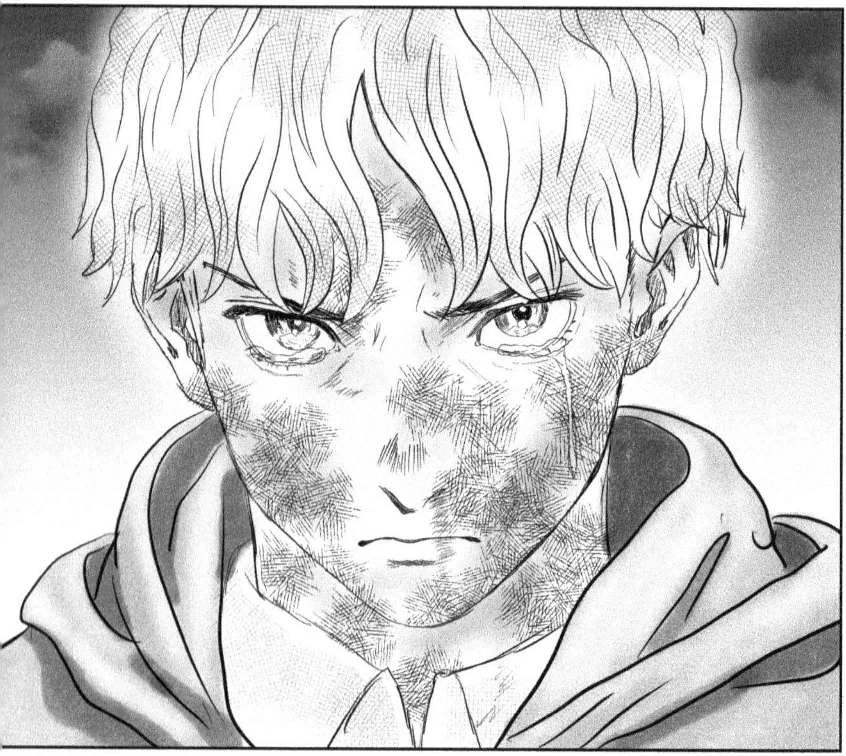

FWOOSH

shake
shake
shake

I DON'T THINK I GET TO SEE TOMORROW

I DON'T THINK I GET TO SEE TOMORROW

HERRGHH!!!!
NICHOLI...

HRAAGH!

...HEGHH
...HEGHH

no....

I CAN GET YOU OUT!

YOU'RE OKAY... THANK GOD
M-M
MARI...

MARI!
YOU'RE OKAY!

DASH

IT'S O-
.....

MARI!

FNOOSH

NICHOLI
!
...

MARI!
MARI CAN YOU HEAR ME!?
trmble trmble

...
PLEASE ANSWER ME

Gasp!
Gasp!

FWOOSH

ARGH!!!!

SNAP
STEP

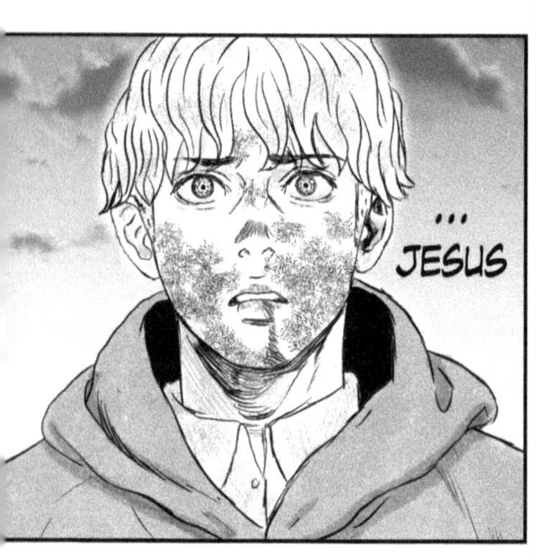

...
JESUS

FWOOSH

PROJECT 100
By Erik Suaste

Chapter 8: Good morning Nicholi

CRUSHER
TO BE CONTINUED

KRRRRK

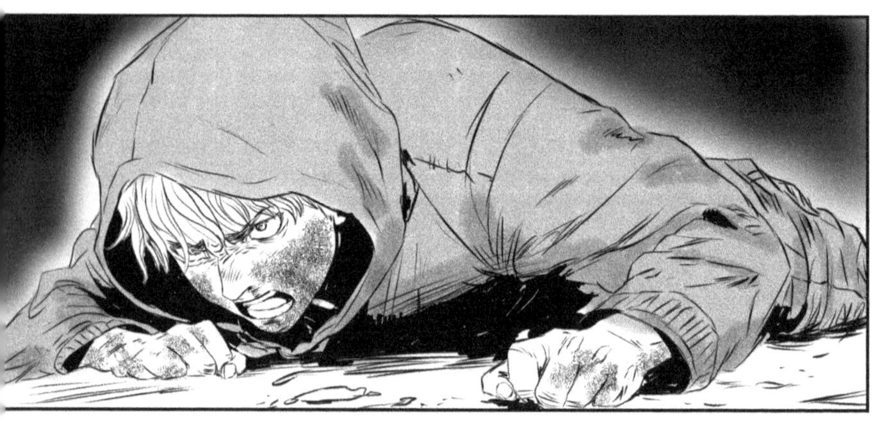

MARI!

BOOOOO

SMACK

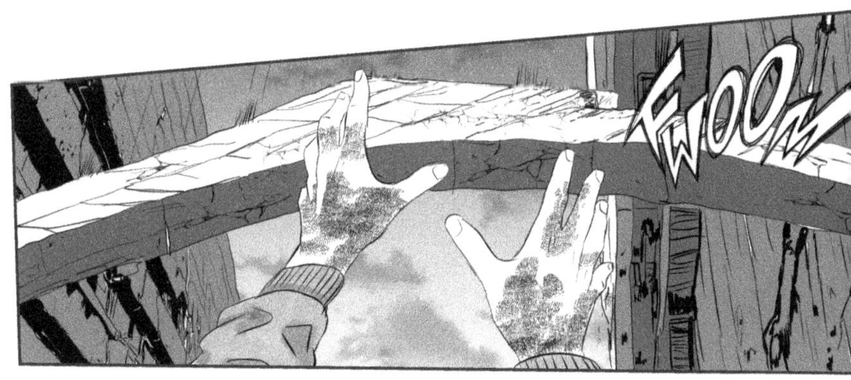
FWOOM

RRRRR
CRAASH

RMMUMBLL
SCIENCE &
TECHNOLOGY

KRAK

VRRRRV

CRACK
CRACK

THUMP THUMP

FWOOM

tumble tumble tumble
VRRRRR

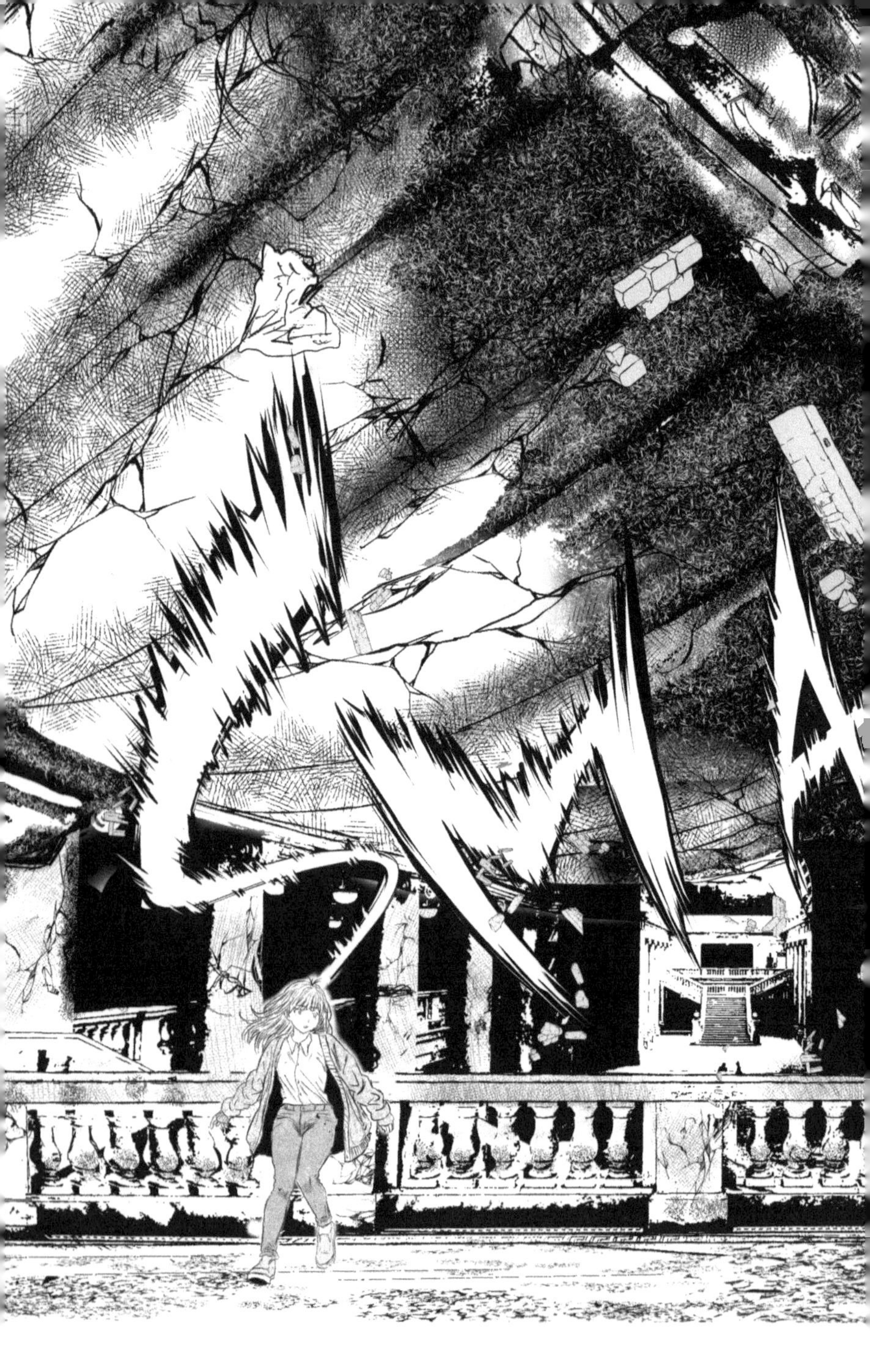

CRAASH

NOOOOOO

NOOOSH

DOOOM

HAUff!
DODGE
Gasp!
Gasp!

BOOM

EVERYONE GET OUT!

CRREEEEEK

RRMMUMBL

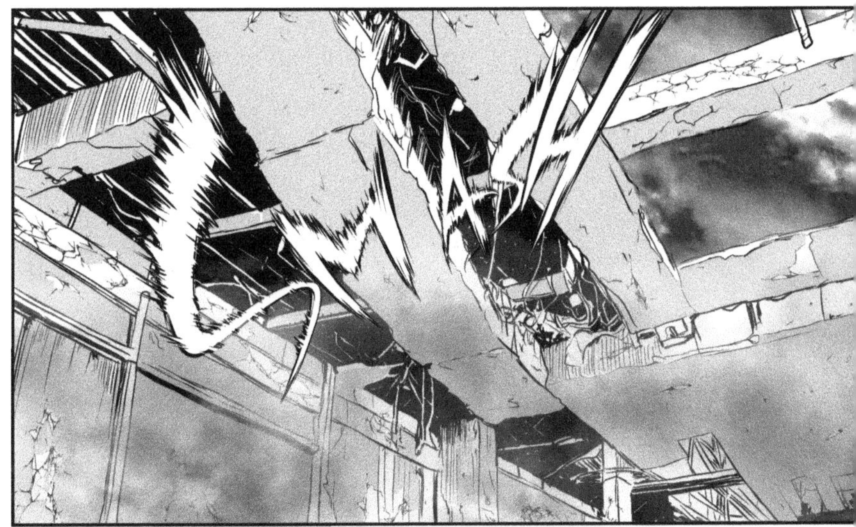

KRA
SH

MARI!

KNOW THAT EVERYTHING FROM THIS POINT IS YOUR FAULT. HUMANITIES FAILURE IS ON YOUR HANDS.
I COULD HAVE SAVED YOU...ALL OF YOU
WHY DIDN'T YOU LET ME?...

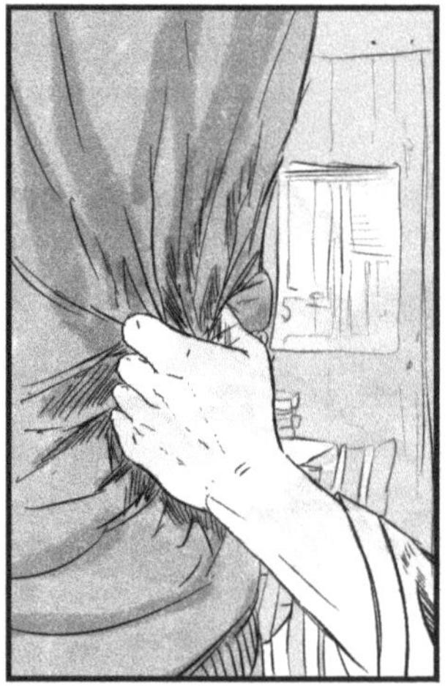

AS ALWAYS...
FOR YOUR OWN SELFISHNESS

CRUNCH!
CRREEEEEK
KAROOO
B
RRMMUMBL!

STOP!

BANG!
BANG!

PING!
PING!

YOU FUCKING MURDERER! NOTHING COULD EVER REDEEM YOU FROM THIS!

NO!

STOP HIM! WE CANT AFFORD LOSING DOCTOR SOREN!

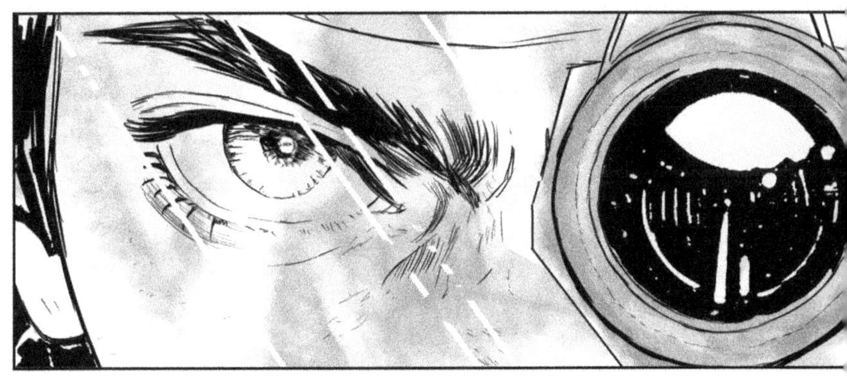

*GASP!

WOOOSH

YOU ABSOLUTE IDIOT!

YOU SINGLE HANDEDLY RUINED EVERYTHING FOR EVERYONE!

BOOOOOM

STOP THAT!
YOU IDIOT !

Wooosh

NO

Chapter 7: Collapsing

PROJECT 100
By Erik Suaste

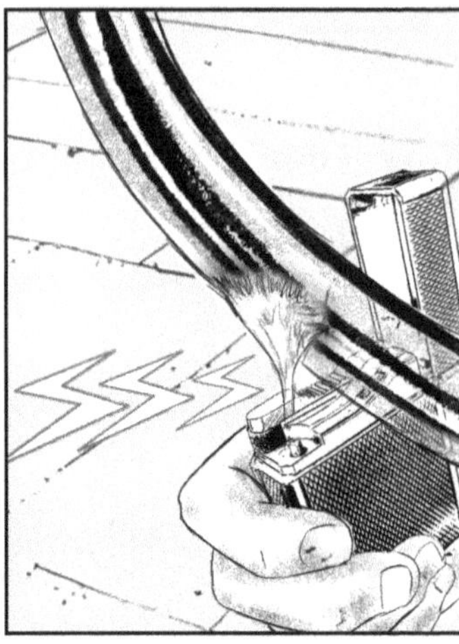

IM
SORRY
...

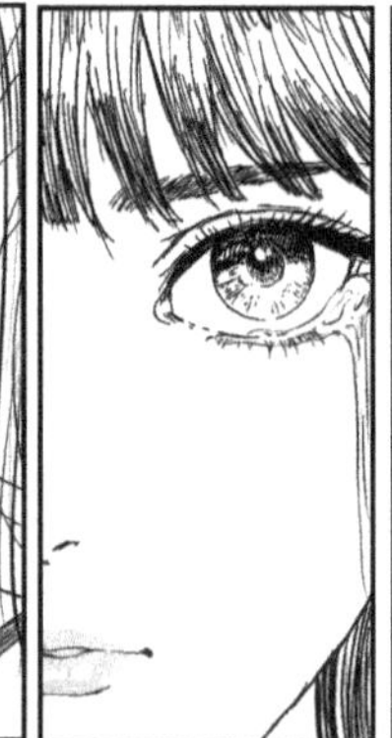

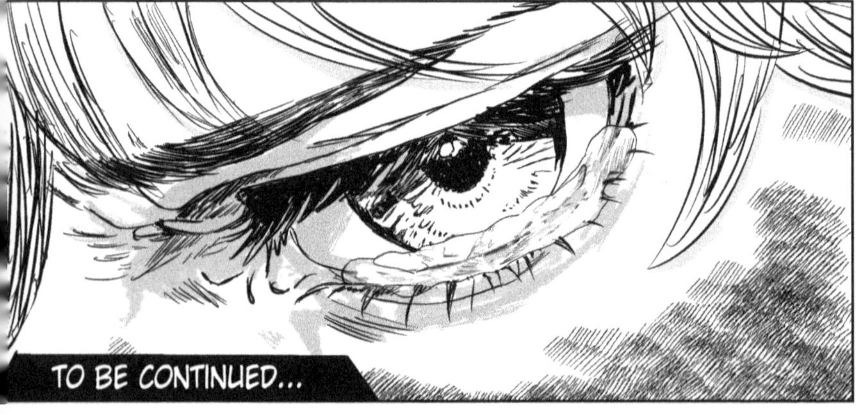
TO BE CONTINUED...

THEN I'LL DO WHAT I CAN...

IF I CAN'T SAVE US...
DANGER
FIRE AND EXPLOSION HAZARD
NO SMOKING OR OPEN FLAMES

ARGHH

I'LL KILL THESE DAMN MONSTERS!

COULDN'T EVEN DEFEND HIMSELF... AND HE THOUGHT HE COULD SAVE HER
WELL, LET'S WRAP THINGS UP, WE'RE FINALLY REACHING THE END AND WE'RE FINALLY STARTING TO GET A WORKING VESSEL...
MAYBE... WE REALLY DO DIE HERE...

THUNK
PING
PING

SUCH A SHAME ... I REALLY HOPED YOU TWO WOULD UNDERSTAND AS LOYAL FOLLOWERS ...
THE MORE YOU STRUGGLE THE WORSE IT IS
NOOOOO! PLEASE, PLEASE! I'M BEGGING YOU!

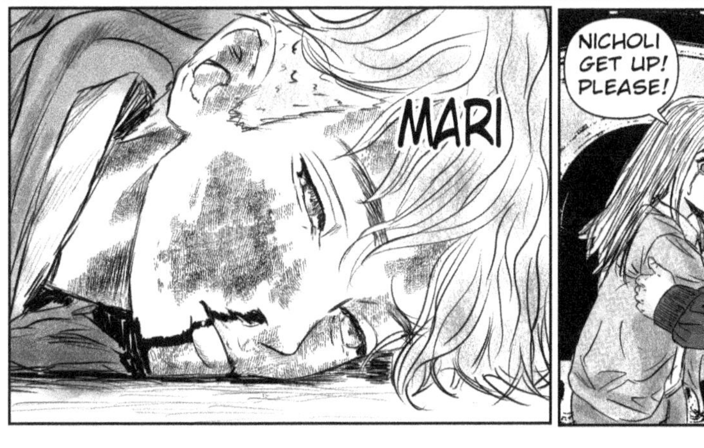

MARI

NICHOLI GET UP! PLEASE!

AGHHH!

WE'RE DONE WITH THESE TWO. YOU KNOW WHAT TO DO, JUST DON'T BE TOO MESSY.

POW

NO! STOP! DONT HURT HE-

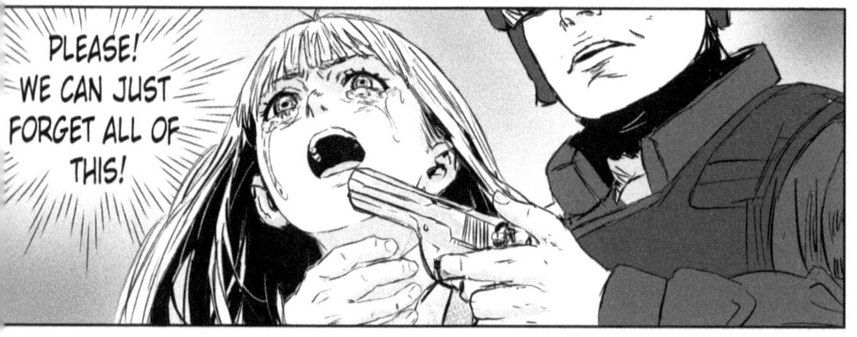
PLEASE! WE CAN JUST FORGET ALL OF THIS!

ALL THIS TIME... THIS IS WHAT IT WAS FOR?

YOU'RE RIGHT... PERHAPS I GOT CARRIED AWAY HAHA

SO WHY ARE YOU TELLING US ALL THIS BULLSHIT! WE NEVER ASKED FOR THIS INFORMATION!
ALL WE WANTED WAS TO BE ABLE TO GO HOME NOT BE A THERAPIST FOR YOU TO DUMP YOUR TRAUMAS!

THEN I SUPPOSE YOUR USEFULNESS HAS RAN OUT

TO FREE OURSELVES FROM OUR OWN HANDS...
WE MUST CUT THEM OFF.

IT'S LIKE PRUNING A TREE, SOMETIMES YOU HAVE TO CUT AWAY A FEW BRANCHES FOR THE WHOLE TO THRIVE.
I'M PREPARED TO SACRIFICE A FEW LIVES TO SAVE TRILLIONS.

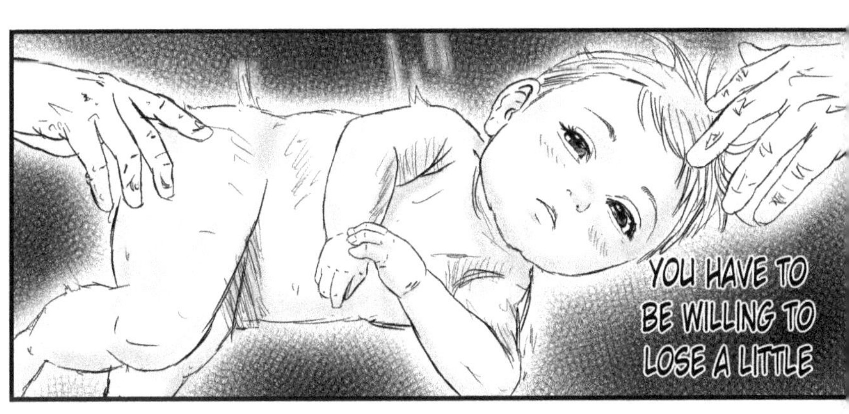

YOU HAVE TO BE WILLING TO LOSE A LITTLE

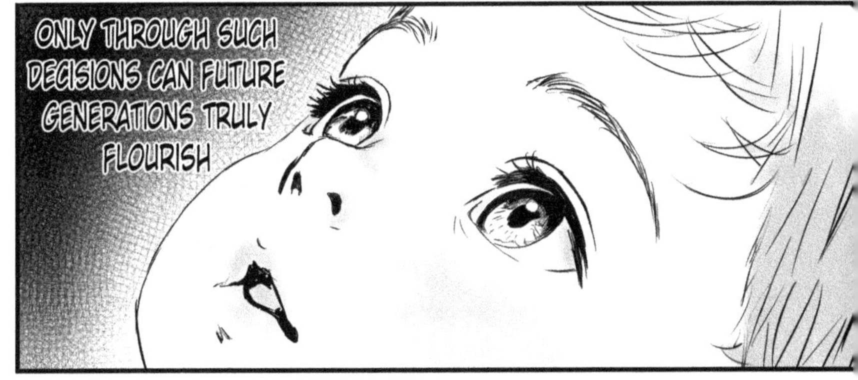

ONLY THROUGH SUCH DECISIONS CAN FUTURE GENERATIONS TRULY FLOURISH

DON'T PUSH AWAY THE NECESSARY CHANGE.

THAT STOPS HERE. IT'S UP TO OUR GENERATION TO TAKE THE BLOW. AND DO WHAT'S RIGHT EVEN IF IT'S BY FORCE

YOU'RE JUST A MURDERER! YOU TAKE CHILDREN FROM THE INNOCENT FOR YOUR LITTLE PROJECT AND WHEN THEY FAIL YOU JUST TOSS THEM LIKE TRASH!

YOU WANT A BETTER WORLD?
THEN LET ME GIVE THAT TO YOU.

SOMETIMES WE JUST HAVE TO DO THE THINGS WE NEVER IMAGINED FOR THE GREATER GOOD...

I SEE YOUR ANGER AND SADNESS BUT THAT'S GOOD BECAUSE THAT TELLS ME YOU'RE GOOD PEOPLE BUT...
I CAN SAVE MORE LIVES THAN YOU CAN COUNT.
...
WHAT DOES THAT MAKE ME?
PAT

IT NEEDS A VESSEL. SOMEONE THAT COULD SAVE US FROM THIS ROTTING PLANET

HOWEVER BY ITSELF IT DOESN'T HAVE MUCH USE...

BUT WHY USE INFANTS! THEY ALREADY HAVE HOMES, PEOPLE WHO CARE FOR THEM!

OBVIOUSLY I CAN'T CREATE MORE VESSELS SO I HAVE TO TAKE THEM FROM SOCIETY, AT RANDOM OF COURSE

EVERY GENERATION THINKS "MY LIFETIME WONT HAVE THE SOLUTIONS, WE'LL LEAVE IT TO THE NEXT."

BUT YOU SEE HUMANS ARE FAR TOO SELFISH...

WE ALL WANT SOLUTIONS SO LONG AS THEY DONT AFFECT US PERSONALLY

BECAUSE WHAT I NEED IS A BLANK CANVAS. PRECONCEPTIONS OF LIFE WILL ONLY SPOIL THE PURPOSE OF THIS BEING. LIFE IS FAR TO UNPREDICTABLE TO LET SOMEONE OF THESE FEATURES GO UNCONTROLLED.

I UNDERSTAND THE PAIN... HOWEVER I AM NO HYPOCRITE. IF I'M USING OTHER'S CHILDREN IT'S BECAUSE I ALREADY TRIED AND FAILED WITH MY OWN

HOWEVER THERE IS A GOOD REASON FOR ALL THIS

I UNDERSTAND MY WORK IS EASY TO CRITICIZE...
I'M WELL AWARE OF IT'S GROTESQUE APPEARANCE

AS I WAS SAYING...

IM SIMPLY DOING WHAT NO ONE ELSE WANTS TO AND I'M WILLING TO COVER MY HANDS IN RED IF IT MEANS A BETTER FUTURE FOR THE YOUTH

AND YET THEY REFUSE TO LOOK AT WHAT IT ACTUALLY TAKES TO FIX THINGS
PEOPLE ALWAYS CRY FOR CHANGE, EXPECTING SOME SORT OF MIRACLE TO APPEAR
you're killing us!
STOP Killing the Planet
LIARS
GIVE US HOPE

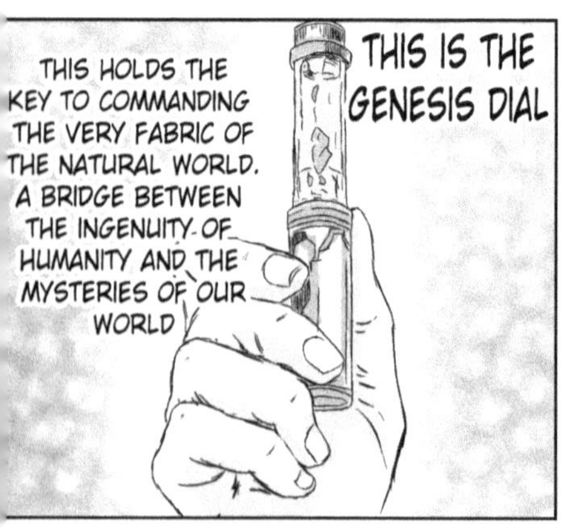

THIS IS THE GENESIS DIAL
THIS HOLDS THE KEY TO COMMANDING THE VERY FABRIC OF THE NATURAL WORLD. A BRIDGE BETWEEN THE INGENUITY OF HUMANITY AND THE MYSTERIES OF OUR WORLD

WE PRAY TO A GOD IN HOPES THAT IT CAN SAVE US AT OUR CONVENIENCE. BUT OUR CALL HAS YET TO BE ANSWERED ALL THIS TIME.
SO IM ANSWERING THE CALL MYSELF AND IM PRESENTING GOD BY MY OWN HANDS.
THIS TANK CARRIES MY LIFES WORK. I'VE MANAGED TO MANIPULATE THE ATOMS IN ELEMENTS AND CONDENSE THEM INTO A VIAL

WHAT THE HELL IS GOING ON IN HERE...

Y'KNOW IVE HAD MY HEAD STUFFED IN MY WORK FOR SO LONG. IVE NEVER ACTUALLY ASKED FOR AN OUTSIDERS OPINION FOR WHAT IM DOING.

AND I KNOW IT CAN LOOK PRETTY BAD BUT IT'S NOT LI-

YOU'RE MONSTERS! WHAT THE HELL HAVE YOU BEEN DOING HERE!?

LISTEN UP EVERYBO[DY]
WE HAVE SOME
GUEST!

DY!

THUFF!

...

BRING THEM IN THE ROOM
...
LETS HAVE A TALK THATS... WORTHWHILE

WHAT...

ARGH!

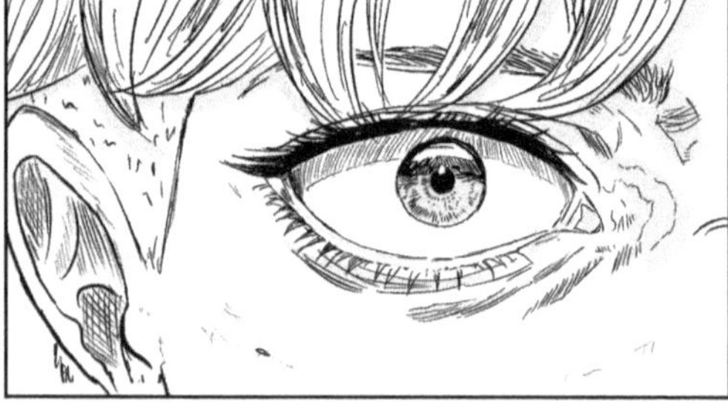

LET GO OF ME!

YOU STAY BACK!

GET YOUR HANDS OFF OF HER!
AGHHH!
WHAT DO YOU WANT TO DO WITH THEM SIR!?

MARI!
I'M COMING!

NICHOLI!

STOP THAT WOMAN RIGHT NOW!

NICHOLI!
MARI!

HEY!

KTANG!

YOU DAMN IDIOT! ALL YOU HAD TO DO WAS GO AROUND THE CORNER!

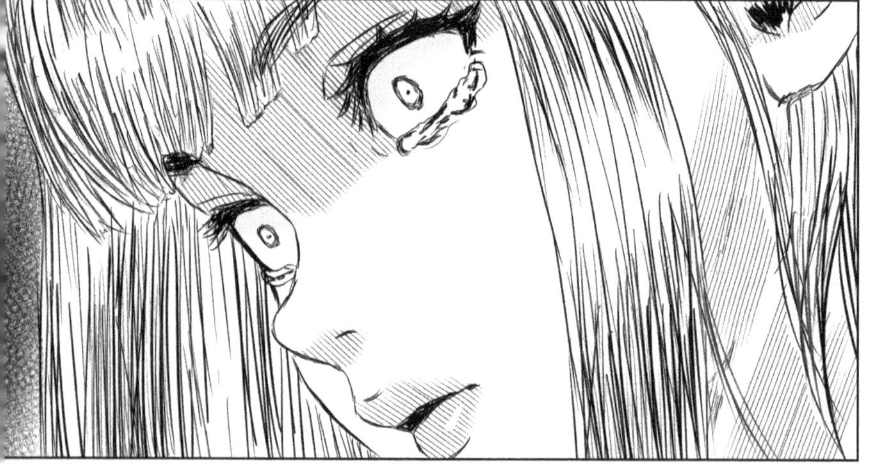

PROJECT100
Chapter 6 In God
we trust
By Erik Suaste

WHAT DID YOU SEE!

HEY!

I'LL JUST BE QUICK!

Tap

TO BE CONTINUED...

THEY WOULDN'T KILL US...

I MEAN WE'RE WITH PHEONIX TECHNICALLY SO WE WOU-

I'M SURE THEY WOULDN'T WANT ANYMORE TROUBLE...

IT'S OKAY...
I WON'T BE
TO FAR...

...

HEY!
HURRY IT UP,
ONE OF YOU
IN HERE.

HOW DO
WE GET
OUT OF THIS
...
SURELY THEY
CAN'T KEEP
UP HERE
FOREVER...

GO TO THE ROOM
DOWN THE
HALLWAY AROUND
THE CORNER.
I'M GONNA SEND
ANOTHER SOLDIER
TO LOOK AFTER YOU
IN A BIT.

I'M GONNA HAVE THEM HELP UNLOAD THE TANKS IN THE ROOMS UP AHEAD.

THAT THE END OF THE LAST BATCH?
ALMOST, PROLLY GOTTA DO A SECOND TRIP. GOT STUCK WITH SOME EXTRAS THOUGH.

Tap Tap
Tap Tap

I'LL GO.

ALRIGHT IMA NEED ONE OF YOU TWO TO HELP UNLOAD IN THIS ROOM. AND THE OTHER HAS TO HELP IN THE ROOM FARTHER DOWN THE HALLWAY.

HEAD UP THESE STAIRS

TMP
TMP
TMP

CRREEEEEK

~SIGH
IT'S A DAMN MIRACLE THIS PLACE IS STILL STANDING TO BE HONEST

AND YOU'RE GONNA STAY HERE UNTIL WE SAY SO.

WELL NO SHIT ... AND YET HERE YOU BOTH ARE

CAN'T HAVE YOU GUY'S POSSIBLY RUNNING YOUR MOUTHS OFF

FUCK ...
I JUST REALIZED THIS OLD ASS BUILDINGS ELEVATORS DEFINITELY DON'T WORK.
BACK TO LIFTING
ANYWAYS THIS SHOULD BE ALL THE TANKS LETS MOVE THEM INSIDE

DIDN'T TAKE LONG FOR IT TO GO TO SHIT.

THE VIEW USED TO BE SO NICE ...

BUT THAT'S WHAT WE'RE HERE FOR RIGHT?
TO BRING BACK WHAT WE LOST.

CLINCK

EXCEPT "WE'RE" NOTHING LIKE YOU MONSTERS.

RRMMUMBL!
LIARS
YEAH... CRAZY DAY...

IT'S BEEN A WHILE SINCE THE CAPITOL WAS RAIDED. FORGOT WHAT IT WAS LIKE UP HERE BEFORE IT WAS ABANDONED.

Tap
Tap

RMMUMBL!
RMMUMBL!

WE'LL SEE ABOUT THAT ...

WE JUST HELP UNLOAD THEM... THEN YOU LET US GO...

UM... FFFINE~ THESE STAIRS JUST MAKES THIS HELLISH

HOW'RE YOU HOLDING UP THERE MARI.

BECAUSE IF YOU WANNA TRY, BE MY FUCKING GUEST.

...AND AFTER SEEING THAT SHIT YOU THINK IT'S A GOOD IDEA TO START GIVING US PROBLEMS?

...

HEY! NO, IT'S FINE WE'LL HELP.

...

THERE'S STAIRS FROM HERE SO WE'RE GONNA HAVE TO LIFT...

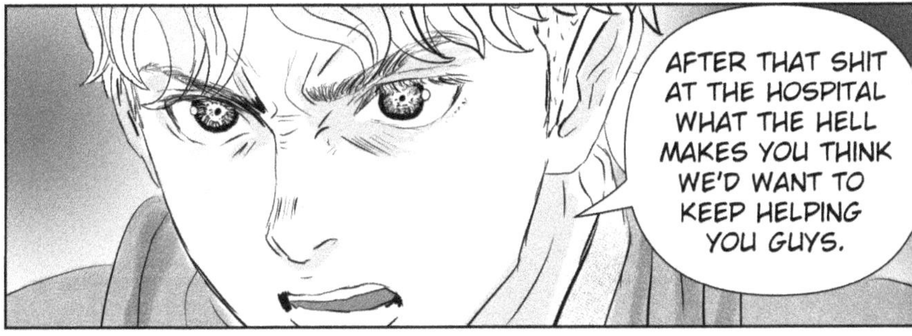

AFTER THAT SHIT AT THE HOSPITAL WHAT THE HELL MAKES YOU THINK WE'D WANT TO KEEP HELPING YOU GUYS.

...

I SEE THE VAN...LOOKS LIKE WE'RE CLEAR OF ANY FOLLOWERS.

...RIGHT... ALRIGHT, WE'LL BE CAREFUL...

SIR WE STILL HAVE GROUP 7 WITH US, HOW DO YOU WANT US TO GO ABOUT THIS...

GET UP, WE'RE HERE... IF YOU'RE GONNA STICK AROUND YOUR GONNA KEEP HELPING.

CRAASH
VROOOM
VROOOM

HOW COULD I
LET ANY OF
THIS HAPPEN

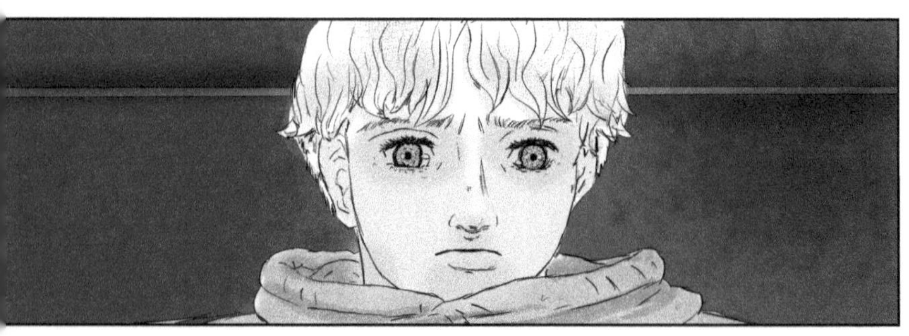

GOD...
WHEN CAN
WE JUST
GET THE
HELL OUT
OF THIS
MESS.

CAPITAL
WE'RE
HEADED
YOUR
WAY WITH
THE
TANKS...

AND SOME
COMPANY...

AGH! LETS JUST GET OUT OF HERE!

I-... DIDNT...

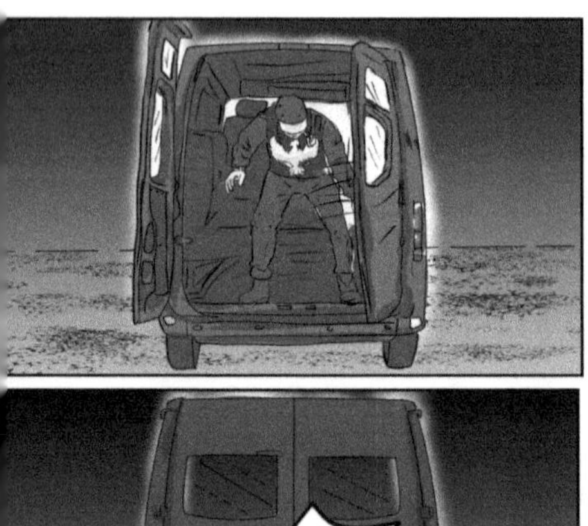

SLAM!

MARI C'MON WE HAVE TO GO!!

Chapter 5: Off Course

BOOOOOM
RRMMUMB
TO BE CONTINUED...

-NATING...-OUT
-PEAT-...
-REA N-
YOU'RE BREAKING OUT.
WE'RE JUST ABOUT
FINISHED SO-
OH FUCK...
GET OUT!

C'MON LET'S JUST LOAD THIS AND GET OUT!

HURRY IT UP!

HEY! HURRY JUST LOAD THIS LAST VAN!
MARI!... MARI!

I HATE TO LEAVE THEM LIKE THIS. BUT WE GOTTA PUT OURSELVES FIRST HERE.

DID YOU SEE WHERE AMY AND LEO WENT?
NO, NOT SURE WHE-

NICHOLI!

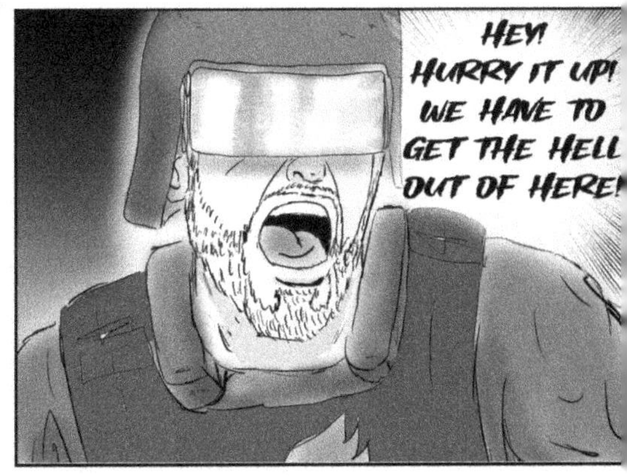

HEY! HURRY IT UP! WE HAVE TO GET THE HELL OUT OF HERE!

NICHOLI!

MARI!
MARI WHERE
ARE YOU!

LEO, IM NOT
SEEING NIC
AND MARI...

BUT YOU SHOULD
DEFINITELY
REACH OUT
ONCE ALL
THIS COMMOTION
IS OVER.

TO BE HONEST,
BEST WE CAN
DO RIGHT NOW
IS HOPE THEY
BEAT US TO
THE DECOY VAN

THIS CAN'T BE GOOD...
WHY WOULD THEY KEEP SOMETHING LIKE THIS FROM US?...

BUT WHAT THE HELL IS IN THOSE BAG'S?..

HURRY, DROP THE EQUIPMENT IN THE CORRESPONDING VAN BEFORE THEY GET TO THIS SIDE!

DAMN, AT THIS RATE WE'RE GONNA GET SEPARATED!

DASH

WE'RE ALMOST TO THE EXI-
BLAM! BANG!
JESUS, THEY'RE STILL GOING AT IT BACK THERE!

BLAM!
BLAM!
BANG!
BANG!

BANG! BLAM! BANG!

HEY, YOU THERE!

CAPITAL! BAGS AND AIR TANKS ARE READY! WE'RE EXITING THE BUILDING SOON!

WE'RE GOING TO PUSH UP AHEAD OF YOU GUY'S AND TRY YO GIVE YOU GUYS A CLEAR EXIT!

WE'RE REACHING THE EXIT! PRIORITIZE GROUP 7!

MARI!? MARI WHERE ARE YOU!?

AGH- NICHOLI!

DAMN... SO MANY OF THEM.

BLAM
...YOU MONSTERS...

ENOUGH! STOP PURSUING ALREADY!

YOU FUCKING MONSTERS WILL PAY FOR THIS IN HELL! DO YOU HEAR ME!

BANG! BANG! BANG!
tremble
tremble
tremble

HURRY! HEAD DOWNSTAIRS!
BANG! BANG!!

STAY THE FUCK DOWN!!

THUNK THUNK
THAT'S SOUNDING LIKE A LOT OF PEOPLE!

THUNK THUNK THUNK
HOLD ON THERE'S PEOPLE COMING DOWN THE STAIRS BEHIND US!

CHANGE OF PLANS HEAD TO THE WEST EXIT!

THEY'RE BEHIND US ALREADY.

WAIT! THOSE ARE PHEONIX LOGOS ON THOSE SOLDIERS!

C'MON WHERE ARE WE GOING!?
...

AAAP
AAAP
AAAP
AAAP
I HEAR YOU! JUST... GIVE ME A SEC!

AAAAP!
AAAAP!
LEO!

LIGHTS ARE OUT! WHERE DO WE GO NEXT!?

AAAAP!
AAAAP!
AAAAP!
AAAAP!
LIGHTS ARE OUT! WHERE DO WE GO NEXT!?

ERRRRRwwwwwwww...
-LETELY SURE...

THE VANS PROBABLY MOVED TO THE OTHER EXIT WE DONT HAVE MUCH TIME TO CATCH IT!

SHIT... HURRY, LET'S GET TO THE OTHER SIDE!

Wooosh

I THINK I KNOW THE WAY FROM HERE, BUT TO BE HONEST I'M NOT COMPL-

YOU KNOW WHICH WAY THE OTHER EXIT IS FROM HERE?!

OH GOD...
WE CANT GO OUT THIS WAY! POLICE ARE OUTSIDE AND I DON'T SEE THE VANS!

BANG!
FUCK!

THEY SHOULD BE! REMEMBER WE GET IN THE DECO-

THE DOORS ARE COMING UP!

STEP
STEP
STEP

STAY CLOSE TO ME MARI!
BLAM! BLAM!
HURRY LET'S GRAB WHAT WE CAN AND GET OUT
BANG! BANG! BANG!
ARE BOTH VANS GONNA BE THERE?
LET'S HEAD TOWARDS EAST EXIT!

THOSE ARE DEFINITELY GUNSHOTS! LEO WHY WOU-
BLAM! BLAM! BLAM!
BANG BANG BANG
THIS HAS NEVER HAPPENED TO US EITHER, I PROMISE YOU!

WHAT THE HELL WAS THAT!?
...THAT WAS DEFINITELY THE FLOOR ABOVE US... 
PROJECT 100
By ERIK SUASTE
Chapter 4: Rush

BLAM! BLAM! BLAM! BLAM!
WOAH!
AAAAAAAAAAAAAA!!!
TO BE CONTINUED...

...WHILE WE HAVE TIME CAN I ASK HOW MUCH DO YOU GUYS REALLY KNOW ABOUT PHEONIX?

ALRIGHT, 5 TANKS LEFT..

THAT, AND WE'VE BEEN ABLE TO GET BIGGER AND BIGGER JOBS. PHEONIX SEEMS TO BE REALLY CONSISTENT WITH THAT. I HEARD RECENTLY THEY'VE EVEN MANA-

WELL IN OUR EXPERIENCE ALL THE HIGHER UP MEMBERS HAVE BEEN COOL WITH US SO FAR.
SO, THATS KINDA WHAT LET OUR TRUST WITH PHEONIX GO UP.

I GUESS WE BETTER GET USED TO THIS SCENERY.

WOW...
THEY DIDNT SKIP A BEAT.
JUST STRAIGHT INTO IT.

YEAHHH

AS IN... ALCOHOL?...

OH?

YA! WE COULD USE SOME MORE FRIENDS TOO, TO BE HONEST.
YOU TRYNA GO OUT FOR DRINKS?

MMMM PERHAPS ~

OH YAYA OF COURSE.
HERE LEMME GET UR NUMBER...

HEY NO WORRIES I DEFINITELY GET WHERE YOU'RE COMING FROM

YEAH, SORRY I SWEAR IM NOT USUALLY THIS TIMID. IT'S JUST THIS IS REALLY OUT OF MY COMFORT ZONE

...
YEAH I MEAN DOIN THIS AT 5 AM ISN'T THE MOST THE RELAXING SETTING HAHA

HEY, AMY...
DO YOU GUY'S DRINK?
!

THIS IS NICHOLI'S 3RD TIME HELPING ME...I THINK. I'VE BEEN DOING THEM FOR ABOUT A YEAR, THOUGH THEY'VE BEEN VERY TINY MISSIONS UNTIL NOW.

SO YOU TWO BEEN DOING MISSIONS FOR A WHILE?

...LOST THE TOUGH GUY ACT PRETTY QUICK...

WE MET WHEN WE GOT PARTNERED TOGETHER FOR A MISSION. HE WAS STOIC AT FIRST BUT ONCE HE OPENED UP HE TURNED ALL SWEET. ISN'T THAT RIGHT~.

WHAT ABOUT YOU GUY'S? HOW'D YOU TWO MEET?
HMM... IT'S BEEN LIKE WHAT? 3 YEARS?

WELL, HERE'S HOPING WE GET TO WORK TOGETHER MORE IN THE FUTURE!

I GUESS THAT'S WHY I CAN'T HELP MYSELF GETTING TO KNOW YOU GUY'S. SEEING YOU TWO REMINDED ME OF HOW WE MET.

. . . .

OOP..

MY NAME IS MARI, AND MR SHY GUY OVER THERE IS NICHOLI

WELL~ SINCE YOU SPOILED MY NAME I MAY AS WELL INTRODUCE US~

HAHA CATS OUT OF THE BAG NOW. YOU GUYS PROLLY KNOW ALREADY BUT IM AMY AND THATS LEONARDO.

WELP, SHE GOT YA THERE

THATS RIGHT! ALL NATURAL BABY!! HAHAHA

HOLD UP LEMME LOCK IN REAL QUICK, HMMPH!
HAHAHA WOWWWW

SO~ FEEL FREE NOT TO ANSWER BUT HOW LONG HAVE YOU TWO BEEN TOGETHER FOR?

OH GOD WHAT IS THIS? HAHAHA

MARI, YOU CAN'T JUST-...
YA! NO WORRIES, WE MET EACHOTHER ABOUT 8 YEARS AGO!

I DUNNO I THINK YOU KINDA GOT IT. I SEEN YOU PUMPING IRON WHEN WE GO TO GYM LATELY.

HERE, GRAB THE OTHER END.

WOWWW OKAY~ HAHAHA JUST GONNA DO ME LIKE THAT INFRONT THE GUEST?

WHAT'RE YOU BENCHING THESE DAYS? 5? 10 POUNDS?

DON'T WORRY I KNOW A THING OR TWO ABOUT GAINZ. I COULD TRAIN YOU

HAHA I MEAN WE CAN ALL USE A LIGHT WORK OUT FROM TIME TO TIME

WELL TO BE HONEST GUYS, I'M PRETTY SURE THESE AREN'T SPARES. SUPPLIES ARE SHORT ENOUGH AS IT IS.
OH SHIT MY BAD HAHA
OH, RIGHT!
HEY~UHH GUYS YOU WANNA START GIVING ME HAND PLEASE. IM NOT EXACTLY BUILT FOR DEADLIFTING AIR TANKS.

OH, NICE CATCH I MISSED IT HEH.
OOP! RIGHT HERE ON THE LEFT!
121

SWEET, LETS GET STARTED. THERE SHOULD BE SOME CARTS THERE TOO TO HELP US LOAD THE TANKS
NO ONES HERE, BUT I DON'T THINK THE TANKS WE'RE GETTING ARE SPARES...

NICE! THE TANKS ARE IN HERE.

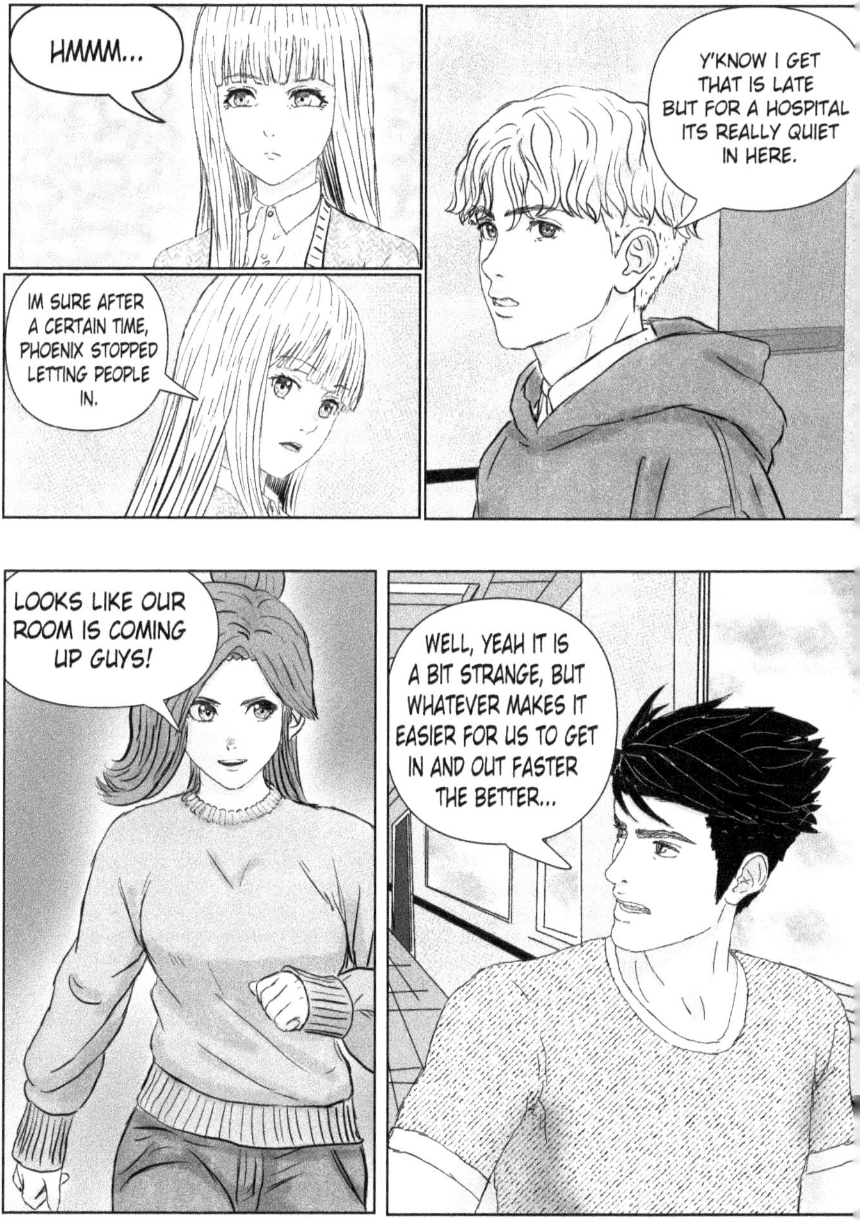

HMMM...
IM SURE AFTER A CERTAIN TIME, PHOENIX STOPPED LETTING PEOPLE IN.
LOOKS LIKE OUR ROOM IS COMING UP GUYS!

Y'KNOW I GET THAT IS LATE BUT FOR A HOSPITAL ITS REALLY QUIET IN HERE.
WELL, YEAH IT IS A BIT STRANGE, BUT WHATEVER MAKES IT EASIER FOR US TO GET IN AND OUT FASTER THE BETTER...

WE COULD USE SOME DOUBLE DATE FRIENDS DONTCHA THINK? EHEHEH
MMMMM
*NUDGE NUDGE
OH! NICE YOU GUYS ARE A COUPLE TOO!
HUH....
ITS SO EMPTY IN HERE...

...

SO~ UHH.. ANYONE HERE ACTUALLY GOOD AT STEALING AIR TANKS?

WELL... IT'S NOT EXACTLY SOMETHING I'D PUT ON THE RESUME TO BE HONEST HEHEH.

ALRIGHT THE ROOM IS 121. SHOULD BE IN THE FIRST FLOOR.

SO HOW'D YOU TWO END UP ON A MISSION LIKE THIS?

WELL, I GUESS TODAY'S GONN BE A FIRST FOR ALL OF US.

THATS RIGHT.
OH! THATS ACTUALLY HOW ME AND LEO MET!

WELL TO BE HONEST I SAW AN OPPORTUNITY TO MAYBE RANK UP WITH PHEONIX EHEH. SO I DRAGGED MY BOYFRIEND WITH ME.

HI! ITS NICE SEEING A FRIENDLY FACE. I'M MA~ I MEAN... UHHH HAHA

ALRIGHT WELL, LET'S HEAD ON IN AND GET STARTED

HMMMPH, SO QUIET OUTSIDE...

HAHA NO WORRIES NAMES AREN'T NECESSARY IF YOU GUY'S AREN'T COMFORTABLE WITH IT.

OH NICE, THEY'RE HERE! OVER HERE GUY'S!
C'MON NOW, HAVE A LITTLE FAITH IN THESE GUYS. WE WERE ALMOST GONNA HAVE TO DO THIS ALONE.

WAS STARTING TO THINK THEY WEREN'T EVEN GONNA SHOW UP.

VROOOOM
University U
Hospital

UNIVERSITY HOSPITAL
KFFFFK

PROJECT 100
By ERIK SUASTE
Chapter 3: Company

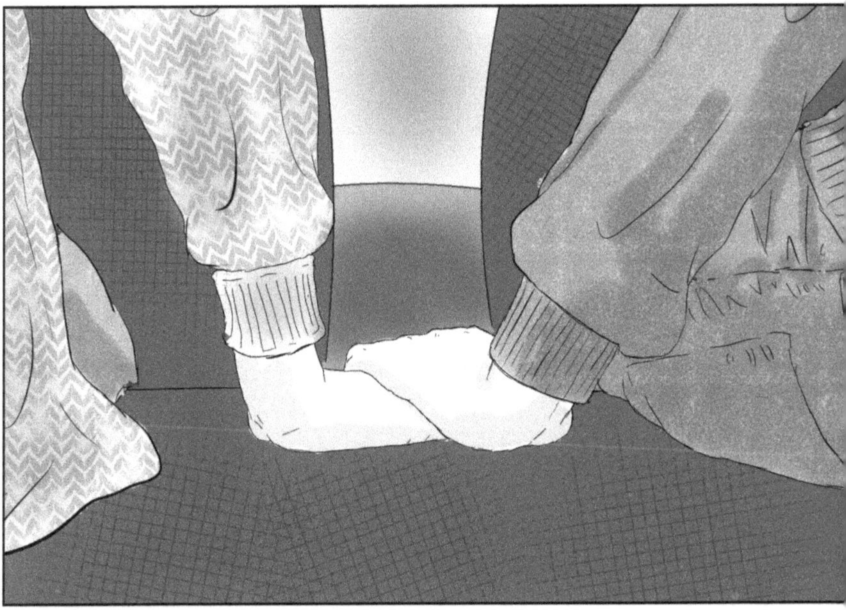

CENTER

TO BE CONTINUED...

BESIDES IF ANYTHING DANGEROUS HAPPENS I'LL JUST COME AND RESCUE YOU! HEHEH
PSHHH, OH YA IM SURE YOU WILL~

IT'S HARD NOT KNOWING WHAT'S AHEAD... BUT ONE THING I DO KNOW IS I'M NOT FACING IT ALONE.
I'VE GOT YOU, AND WE'VE GOT EACH OTHER.

ALRIGHT, WELL LET'S JUST HOPE EVERYTHING GOES BY SMOOTHLY
WE'LL BE OKAY

HEY

*SIGH~

I GET THAT YOU'RE ANXIOUS...
BUT LIFE'S KINDA MESSY LIKE THAT.
WE'VE MADE IT THROUGH
EVERYTHING SO FAR SIDE BY SIDE,
AND WE'RE GONNA HANDLE
THIS TOO.

GROUP 7?
YEAH, THATS US.
BY THE TIME WE GET THERE
SOME THINGS WILL ALREADY
BE GOING ON.
SO YOU'LL WANNA TRY AND
BLEND IN WITH ALL THE
COMMOTION.
ALRIGHT, I'M GONNA
DROP YOU GUYS
OFF AT THE
WEST ENTRANCE.
THATS THE PLAN.

MMM WELL OUR RIDE SHOULD BE HERE BY NOW. HOPEFULLY EVERYTHING GOES BY SMOOTHLY.
tmp tmp tmp

YEAH, I GET IT. IT'S NOT THE KIND OF MISSION I WOULD HAVE EVER EXPECTED. BUT SOMETIMES WE HAVE TO DO THE THINGS WE NEVER IMAGINED FOR THE GREATER GOOD.
HMM, I CAN'T HELP BUT FEEL A BIT UNEASY ABOUT ALL THIS. SNEAKING INTO A HOSPITAL, STEALING THINGS, ... IT JUST DOESN'T SIT RIGHT WITH ME

WE'RE DOING WHAT WE CAN WITH THE INFORMATION WE HAVE. IM SURE PHEONIX WOULDN'T BE DOING THIS IF THEY DIDN'T THINK IT WAS NECESSARY. BESIDES SOMETIMES YOU GOTTA GET YOUR HANDS DIRTY IF YOU'RE TRYNA CLEAN UP A MESS.
I KNOW, I KNOW IT'S JUST HARD TO SHAKE OFF THE GUILT. JUST A LITTLE WORRIED IF WE'RE CAUSING MORE HARM INSTEAD OF HELPING.

I KNOW, IT'S A TOUGH SITUATION. I WON'T DENY THAT. BUT I'M PUTTING MY TRUST IN PHOENIX AS USUAL. BESIDES IT'S BETTER OFF IN OUR HANDS WHERE WE CAN MAKE SURE THOSE RESOURCES GO WHERE THEY'RE TRULY NEEDED.
TRUE, BUT I CAN'T HELP BUT THINK ABOUT THE PEOPLE IN THAT HOSPITAL, THE ONES WE'RE ESSENTIALLY TAKING FROM. WHAT IF WE'RE STEALING FROM THOSE WHO NEED IT THE MOST.

STEP
STEP

I'M GOOD,
A LITTLE SAD
OUR ROLE FEELS
A BIT MINISCULE
BUT WE'RE HELPING
REGARDLESS I'M SURE.

SO...
HOW ARE YOU
FEELING?

Fwoosh

I KNOW IT MAY SEEM AS IF WE HAVE SMALL ROLES, BUT KNOW THAT WITHOUT THE SMALL GEARS AND COGS, THE MACHINE THAT IS PHOENIX WOULDN'T WORK WITHOUT YOUR HELP.

AT SOME POINT WE WILL SEE THE IMPACT OF OUR ACTIONS. I ONLY WISH I COULD TELL YOU WHEN...
UNTIL THEN STAY SAFE. I HOPE TO SEE YOU ALL RETURN FOR FUTURE MISSIONS. REMEMBER, THE FUTURE IS OURS TO CREATE. GOOD LUCK OUT THERE.

OUR GOAL IS TO GATHER OUR GROUPS MATERIAL FROM THE S.L.C HOSPITAL, THEN DROP IT OFF AT THE CURRENT PHEONIX HQ, WHICH IS AT THE STATE CAPITOL
Utah State Capitol
we are here
salt lake city hospital
Salt Lake City
CENTRAL CITY
EAST CENTRAL

AFTER THAT, EVERYTHING ELSE WILL BE TAKEN CARE AT THE CAPIITOL. AND YOU GUYS SHOULD BE GOOD FOR THE NIGHT.
WE DROP OFF GROUP 7 ON THE WEST ENTRANCE. ONCE YOUR ITEMS ARE COLLECTED YOU'LL DROP OFF YOUR ITEMS IN THE CAPITOL VAN AT THE EASTERN ENTRANCE.
Huntsman Parking
salt lake city hospital
W
N
S
E
THERE WILL BE ANOTHER VAN THERE AS WELL. THAT VAN WILL WORK AS AN ESCAPE VEHICLE/DECOY TO HELP THE MAIN VAN ESCAPE. YOU WILL ALSO BE LEAVING IN THAT ESCAPE VAN.
University College of Nursing

YOU'LL BE GETTING PICKED UP BY ONE OF OUR DRIVERS IN A COUPLE MINUTES. FROM HERE THEY'LL BE TAKING YOU TWO TO THE S.L.C HOSPITAL.
WOOSH

...LET'S GO OVER THE MAP. CAN YOU GRAB THE OTHER SIDE FOR ME KARI?
*TAP
* TAP

SWOOSH!

ALRIGHT KARI WE'RE PRETTY MUCH WRAPPED UP OVER HERE SO LETS START CLOSING THIS UP.

YOU SHOULD BE GLAD YOU'RE EVEN ALLOWED TO JOIN. CONSIDERING HOW LATE YOU EVEN SHOWED UP!
LOOK, JUST MEET UP WITH AMY AND LEONARDO... YEAH I THINK THAT'S THEIR NAMES.
RIGHT, YEAH NO, IT'S FINE! BESIDES THE SOONER WE'RE BACK HOME THE BETTER RIGHT MARI~

ALRIGHT BOYS, LET'S GET OVER TO THIS SIDE.
TO KEEP THINGS MORE FOCUSED BRUNO WILL QUICKLY GO OVER GROUP 6 AND WHAT THEIR MISSION IS AND WE'LL GO OVER OURS SEPARATELY.

OKAY, THE GOAL FOR THE TWO OF YOU IS TO MEET UP WITH GROUP 5 ON THE WEST SIDE OF THE BUILDING AND SECURE AS MANY OXYGEN TANKS AS YOU CAN. GROUP 5 WILL HAVE MORE DETAILS. GET IN AND OUT. THE LESS YOU INTERACT THE BETTER.

WAIT, ALL THIS JUST TO PICK UP SOME AIR TANKS? ISN'T THERE ANYTHING A LITTLE BIGGER WE CAN DO?

THE HOSPITAL?...
THESE TWO GROUPS WILL BE FOCUSING ON GRABBING THE MATERIALS NECESSARY FROM THE S.L.C HOSPITAL AND BRINGING THEM TO PHEONIX'S CURRENT HQ.

NOW IT'S LIKELY YOU'LL RUN INTO OTHER MEMBERS FROM DIFFERENT GROUPS BUT THEIR GOALS ARE COMPLETELY DIFFERENT THAN YOURS, SO ITS IMPORTANT YOU STAY IN YOUR LANE NO MATTER WHAT.

AS YOU CAN TELL WE'RE LOW ON PEOPLE FOR THIS JOB. TONIGHT WE'RE WORKING AS A SMALLER PART OF A BIGGER HEIST.
YOU'LL BE CATEGORIZED IN GROUPS 1 THROUGH 7. THESE RANKS ARE FROM MOST IMPORTANT TO LEAST.

ALRIGHT, WELL LET'S GATHER ROUND AND WE'LL BREAK DOWN THE RULES OF THIS PLAN.

HOWEVER ONLY TWO OF THOSE GROUPS ARE MEETING HERE. THAT BEING 6 AND 7, THE TWO LOWEST.
6
7

DAMN, WE'RE DEAD LAST

C'MON KARI DONT BE SO COLD. DON'T WORRY ABOUT IT, IT'S ALL GOOD. WE'RE GLAD YOU EVEN SHOWED UP TO BEGIN WITH.

SORRY, IT'S JUST WE CAME FROM DIFFERENT AREAS SO WE ENDED UP TAK-
GEEZ

NICE TO MEET YOU. WELL IM GLAD IT WORKED OUT HEHEH.

ANYWAYS I'M BRUNO, I LEAD OUR DIVISION. AND THAT'S MY CO-LEAD KARI. WE'RE A BIT LOW ON PEOPLE TONIGHT BUT WE CAN USE ANY HELP WE CAN GET. SO IF YOU'RE LATE CAUSE YOU WANNA BRING HELP, IT'S FINE BY ME.

YOU DO THAT AGAIN AND YOU WON'T BE SEEING ANOTHER MISSION.
TOOK EM LONG ENOUGH ...
OH! NICE THEY'RE HERE!

PROJECT 100
By ERIK SUASTE
ALRIGHT IT SHOULD BE ON THE ROOFTOP.
Chapter 2: movement

C'MON THEY'RE PROBABLY JUST WAITING FOR US.
JESUS MARI, HOW ARE YOU SO CARELESS.

HMMM
I WONDER HOW MANY NEW PEOPLE THERE ARE THIS GO AROUND SINCE THIS SEEMS LIKE A BIGGER JOB.

WELL I'M TRUSTING IN THEM THROUGH YOU SO HOPEFULLY THINGS CAN GO WELL
AND IT SEEMS LIKE PHOENIX IS THE ONLY ACTUAL GROUP THAT SEEMS CLOSE ENOUGH TO BRING CHANGE.
OOO! THIS IS THE SPOT

OKAY, THIS SHOULD BE THE MEET UP POINT.
MAN~ OF COURSE IT'S GOTTA LOOK LIKE THIS.
TO BE CONTINUED

AND YEAH... TECHNICALLY THIS STUFF IS ILLEGAL BUT IF NOT PEOPLE LIKE US, THEN WHO ELSE?
...ALL MY OTHER "MISSIONS" WERE SMALL BUT THIS TIME THEY'RE WILLING TO LET ME TAKE ON SOMETHING BIGGER!
YEAH! AND IF WE DECIDE TO HAVE KIDS SOMEDAY I DON'T WANT TO FEEL LIKE I'M LEAVING THEM SOMEWHERE BAD
YEAH I MEAN ANYTHING TO HELP THE NEXT GENERATION IM SURE IS WORTH IT

YOU KNOW I DON'T MIND HELPING YOU WITH THESE KINDS OF THING'S BUT HOW MUCH DO YOU EVEN KNOW ABOUT THIS ORGANIZATION?
I MEAN, WHY 4AM?
I CANT HELP BUT OVERTHINK ...
SIGH~ ALRIGHT, SORRY IT'S JUST A BIT SPOOKY DOING THIS SO LATE. I DUNNO HOW YOU DO IT.
WELL, I KNOW IT SEEMS ODD BUT YOU KNOW HOW STRICT THE GOVERNMENT IS ABOUT PEOPLE INTERFERING WITH THE ENVIRONMENT.
I KNOW I PROBABLY CANT DO MUCH BUT EVEN IF IT'S JUST A LITTLE I HAVE TO HELP
BUT ITS CLEAR THE WORLDS HEALTH IS REACHING IT'S LIMITS AND IT DOESN'T SIT RIGHT WITH ME.

FEELS LIKE WE'RE SO LONG OVERDUE MOVING IN TOGETHER
BUT ONCE WE'RE FINALLY SETTLED WE CA-
HEY C'MON NOW, YOU'VE DONE SO WELL LETS MAKE SURE YOU STICK WITH YOUR PROMISE AND ACTUALLY STOP THIS TIME.
AH-!
SWIPE!

HAHA WELL I GUESS YOU'RE RIGHT. LET'S GET GOIN
WELL~ AT LEAST I'M WITH YOU NOW, WHICH IS MUCH BETTER.
WELL I GOT MOST OF YOUR THINGS OUT AND SOME OF THE KITCHEN.
SO HOW MUCH WERE YOU ABLE TO UNPACK TODAY?
AHH DONT WORRY ABOUT IT. IF I HAD TO UNPACK IT ALL BY MYSELF JUST TO MAKE SURE WE FINALLY LIVE TOGETHER, I'M MORE THAN HAPPY TO.
NICE!... AGAIN SORRY I COULDN'T HELP TODAY. YOU KNOW HOW MY DAD GETS WHEN MOM WAN-

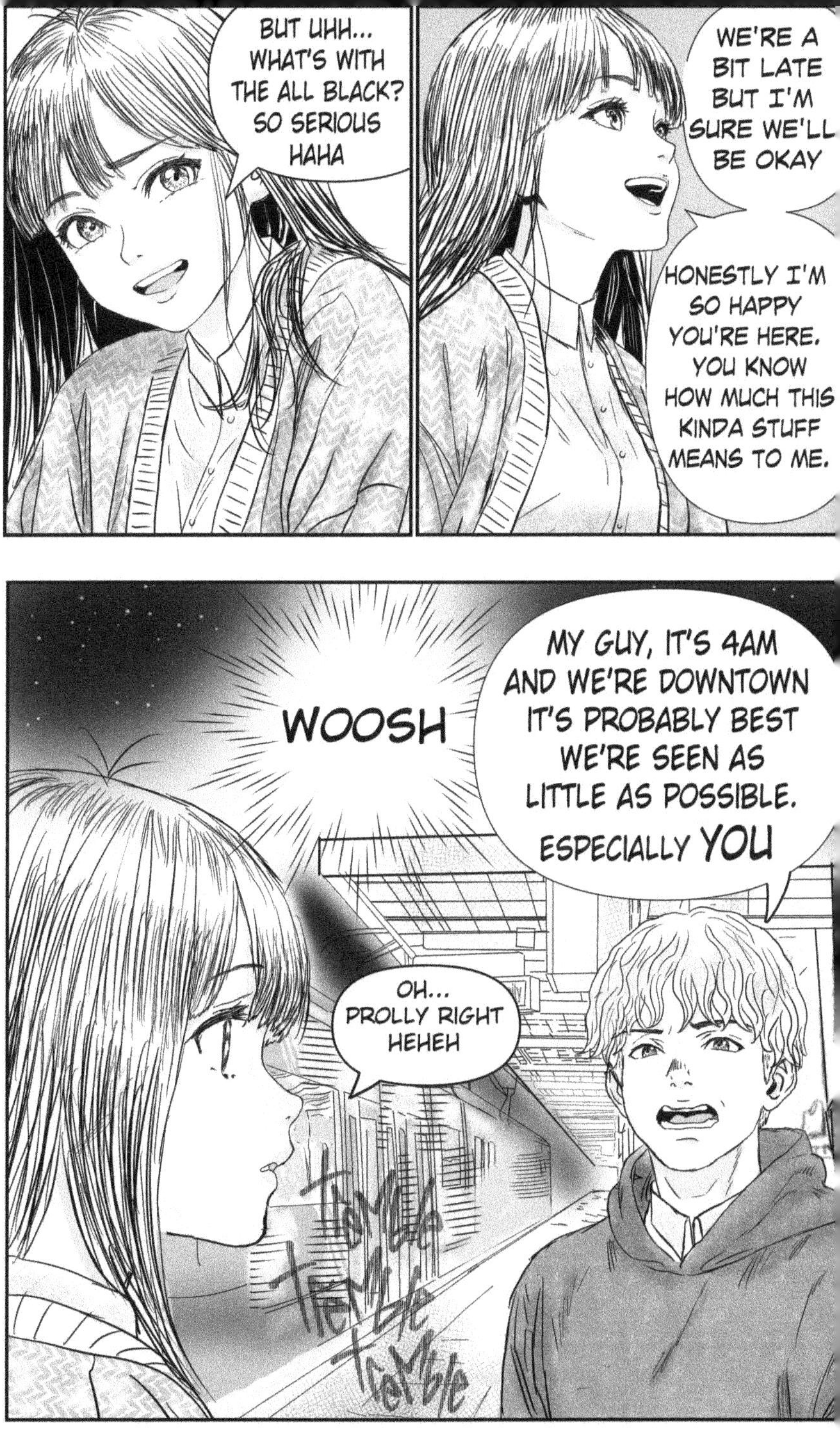

BUT UHH... WHAT'S WITH THE ALL BLACK? SO SERIOUS HAHA
WE'RE A BIT LATE BUT I'M SURE WE'LL BE OKAY
HONESTLY I'M SO HAPPY YOU'RE HERE. YOU KNOW HOW MUCH THIS KINDA STUFF MEANS TO ME.
WOOSH
MY GUY, IT'S 4AM AND WE'RE DOWNTOWN IT'S PROBABLY BEST WE'RE SEEN AS LITTLE AS POSSIBLE. ESPECIALLY YOU
OH... PROLLY RIGHT HEHEH

welcome to salt lake city
ALLEY
NICHOLI!
OVER HERE!
HEY! THANKS FOR COMING WITH ME.

PROJECT 100

ERIK SUASTE

STEP
STEP

SIGH~

TMP
TMP
TMP

BZZZ!

4:31 AM
Mari
I have an alarm set no worries
8:43 PM
Almost at the train station cya in a bit <3
4:31 AM
New

BZZZZT

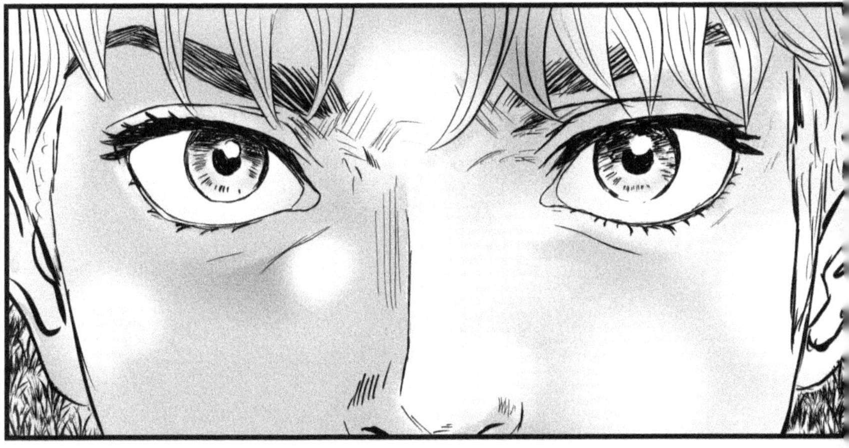

TMP
TMP
TMP

STEP
STEP

S-SORRY!
AH-!
THUD

EEGHHH

. . .

I'M SORRY
BROTHER... HELP ME OUT

AHHHGHH YOU PRICK!

GIO'S BEER!
*COUGH COUGH

HERRGHH!

STEP

Chapter 1: For you.

Theres something beautiful in creating
something that almost breaks you,
There's both pride
and frustration in this work and yet
all of it is real,
Project 100 is my heart on the page,
I hope it reaches yours.
-Erik Suaste